by
Earl Baldwin
Peter dePaolo
and
Frank Frazetta

This edition of JOHNNY COMET © 1991 Eclipse Books
art © 1991 Frank Frazetta

Published by Eclipse Books
Post Office Box 1099, Forestville, California 95436.

softcover ISBN: 1-56060-010-1
clothcover ISBN: 1-56060-009-8

edited by Letitia Glozer and Dean Mullaney
book design by Michael Dashow
title logo by Steve Vance
art and lettering touch-ups by
Michael Dashow, Miyako Graham, Cat Yronwode, and C. Moi
cover coloring by Steve Oliff

## EDITOR'S NOTE

Attempting a reprint project of this size is a difficult task; no one truly realized how difficult until the gears had been set in motion. Assembling almost four hundred individual strips thirty-eight years after their initial, rather limited publication was a daunting task that could not have been accomplished without the gracious help of scholars, art collectors, and friends. Whenever possible, Frank Frazetta's original art was used to ensure the best reproduction possible. When originals were unavailable, printer's proofs, photocopies, or actual clipped newspaper strips (including some truncated, two-tier Sunday strips) were used. We regret that reproduction quality varies in the volume even though every effort was made to provide as attractive and complete a reprinting of *Johnny Comet* as could be assembled.

Eclipse Books wishes to thank Russ Cochran, John Cosgriff, Jack Gilbert, Ted Hanes, Topper Helmers, Rick Hoppe, Tom Horvitz, Albert Moy, Ethan Roberts, Chris Rock, James Silk, Lance Suarez, Jim Sullivan, Greg Theakston, Michael Thibodeaux, John L. Watson, Bob Wiacek, Bill Wray, Berni Wrightson, and those donors who asked to remain anonymous, for the use of their art.

Special thanks go to Bill Blackbeard of the San Francisco Academy of Comic Art, Wally Harrington, and William Stout for use of original art and archival material from their collections, as well as constant and gracious assistance throughout this project.

—Letitia Glozer

## PUBLISHER'S NOTE

Although "ghost" artists are not credited in newspaper strips, astute art-spotters always notice when a feature suddenly acquires a new look, and many also enjoy guessing the identity of the unnamed renderer who has pencilled or inked the strip while the regular artist is on vacation, sick, or trying to catch up to deadlines.

Frazetta fans will notice that throughout the run occasional *Johnny Comet* strips bear the marks of helper-artists, and that beginning with the dailies and Sundays for December, 1952, Frank received extensive assistance from one or more ghosts whose style differed markedly from his.

Al Williamson, Frank's good friend at the time, remembers one hectic day when he helped the deadline-crunched Frazetta produce an entire week's worth of *Johnny Comet* dailies in just four hours. He also recalls illustrator Jack Hearne helping out at a later date. Rather than spoil your puzzle-solving fun by revealing the name of a third ghost artist, we will simply state that those who know their ECs will know *at once* who he was when they see his work.

The rest of you may be stumped, but if you are curious, just scrutinize the Sundays for January 4th and 18th, 1953 (pages 218 and 220). On each of them you will receive an impeccably lettered and very quiet "hello" from across the gulf of lost years.

Frank had some fine pals, you know?

—cat yronwode & Dean Mullaney

# CONTENTS

# Let's Set the Record Straight

## by Nick Meglin

Can someone be totally objective about a close friend's art? Depending upon the work, the circumstances, the relationship, and a hundred other complex factors, I can answer that question with a firm, strong, unequivocal "maybe."

As for myself, vis-à-vis the work of Frank Frazetta, I wouldn't try. A totally objective approach would entail separating the man from his work. Well, I've seen Frank work, I've seen him play, and I've seen him play at work. It's one and the same. His primary goal is fun, and he is as intense on a baseball diamond as he is at the drawing board, but never at the expense of his playfulness.

Years back, following our Saturday morning softball ritual in a Brooklyn schoolyard, Frank, Angelo Torres, and I were scanning *Johnny Comet* daily and Sunday originals. Ange pointed to a particular panel and complimented Frank on the way he had set up the dramatic conflict.

"I exaggerated the light and shade so that the darks emphasized the tensions in Comet's face," Frank explained. "Then I punched it up even further by placing a flat black behind him. His black shirt blended into the background so his expression became the focal point."

"This other character you created is great," I added.

"Oh, I didn't create him, that's my Uncle Louie!"

Ange and I broke up. That little exchange showed Frank at his typical best—drama, mood, action, tension—a serious film director on paper, but not taking himself so seriously that he couldn't have a little fun with his Uncle Louie! And while his youthful spirit and exuberance pervades everything he does, these are the very vital elements invariably missing from so much of what has been written about him. When a person becomes as much legend as man, as has Frank Frazetta, far too many need to believe the man can be summed up by his work alone. They try to validate their beliefs with utter nonsense, transforming—albeit in their own minds—opinion to fact. The trouble is, of course, that "fact" seems to be inherent in the printed word. And their distortions have filtered through the public strainer to make that transformation credible to a considerable degree.

A case in point would be the article about Frazetta that appeared in *Esquire* years ago. I read it and called Frank immediately. Before hearing his own reaction to the piece, I told him that it "was about time somebody actually topped your extensive imagination with their own. Or had I missed the point? Were these flights of fancy intended to be taken as comedy of the absurd?"

Frank was less amused. He asked me, as a writer more than friend, to explain to him "how someone could come to my home, visit with me, look around, ask questions, and then write a piece of sheer fiction like that?" In sensing how deeply hurt he was, I offered a professional appraisal. I told him perhaps the key word here wasn't "how" but "why." It might be that the writer was insensitive, stupid, cruel, untalented, and perhaps all of the above, or—and this was the saddest possibility of all—maybe that was his assignment, a dictum handed down by his editor: "Let's get the legend." After all, iconoclasm sells a lot more magazines than the mundane! No one wants to hear that Frank Frazetta is a family man who is deeply devoted to his wife and kids, not when there's a painting on the wall showing some primitive war lord wielding a golden sword. Why print that the artist, in his own real world, wields only a baseball bat, and not to crush a band of wild apes but to send a benign baseball over the left field fence?

That article was similar to others in approach—better to suggest that the craggy rocks and gnarled trees depicted in a Frazetta painting represent a dark outlook on a chaotic world; barbarians portray violence as a method of dealing with violence in a violent world, the sword...well, anyone who took Psych 101 or reads Ann Landers religiously knows what *that* means! Forget the inconsequential detail that Frazetta was illustrating a Conan adventure at the time. (Consider it lucky they weren't dissecting

Frank's love of baseball. Bats, balls, the "diamond" shape…talk about having a "field" day!)

While the *Esquire* fiasco reached a wider public, they were nameless and faceless. What of the countless bits and pieces appearing in fanzines and newsletters that circulated about? These were not nameless, faceless people, but fans, art students, imitators, and supposed friends. Frank was always a generous man, giving of himself willingly and unhesitatingly, never measuring nor expecting reciprocity. Thus, his very accessibility became his own vulnerability. Several of those who experienced Frank's graciousness became chief offenders and the body of trash they invented was obviously the result of pure jealousy. Oh, how the two-faced revel in knocking gods off the pedestals they themselves erect.

In the 35-plus years I've known him, I've never heard Frank pontificate or take an exalted position (deserving as he has been to do so). He lives a simple existence and simple are his needs and pleasures. He is also a natural talent at everything he does and nothing fans the flames of jealousy more than seemingly effortless achievement, which is why it's easy to make analogies between Frazetta's artistic and athletic abilities…

…Grasping a mottled pencil stump, Frank's hand sweeps across the page and in bold, quick strokes captures the gesture, mood, character—the essence—of the human form posed before him in just a few seconds' time.

…Dipping a steel nib into India ink, he uses delicate, intricate pen strokes to define dynamic figures that exist only in the caverns of his vivid imaginative world.

…Clutching a bat, he stands at the plate like a coiled spring. And when he releases his energy in a fluid, graceful swing, you need only hear the crack of impact to know that the ball is gone.

The world is full of imitators, but the originals, the "naturals," the Frank Frazettas, come few and far between.

About this, I can be totally objective!

Promotional strip, January 26, 1952

# Frank Frazetta:
# A Brief Introduction

## by Wally Harrington

The year was 1952. President Harry Truman sat in the White House; the Army sat in Korea. The New York Yankees beat the Brooklyn Dodgers to win the World Series, and Troy Ruttman won the Indianapolis 500.

Among other, less heralded events of that year was the advent of a newspaper strip titled *Johnny Comet*, written by Peter DePaolo and illustrated by Frank Frazetta, which made its first appearance on Monday, January 28.

Frank Frazetta was born in Brooklyn, New York, on February 9, 1928. From childhood on, he displayed exceptional artistic ability. In elementary school he created several comic books with his own cast of characters, which caught the attention of adults around him. Frazetta's third grade teacher convinced the boy's parents to provide formal art training, and Frazetta was enrolled in Brooklyn's Academy of Fine Arts at the tender age of eight, studying with Michael Falanga, an artist of the classical Italian school. With but three rooms, Falanga's school accommodated but thirty students, with Frazetta the only non-adult enrolled.

Falanga, taken with the child prodigy's ability, insisted Frazetta's parents send him to Italy for more formal study. However, Falanga died before the trip could be arranged. Upon his death, the school was closed and Frazetta returned to the Brooklyn school system for the rest of his education.

As a teenager Frazetta began to display another amazing talent: while he could draw very well, he could hit a baseball even better. He had continued drawing but, growing up in a tough area of Brooklyn where art was considered "sissy," his drawing began to take a back seat to baseball. While attending Lincoln High School, he was offered a contract with the New York Giants and had to decide whether to play ball or continue studying art.

Fortunately for us, Frazetta decided against baseball and

began his career as an artist in December 1944, at the age of 16, working as an assistant to John Giunta, perhaps best known for his work on *Blackhawk*. Frazetta's first solo endeavor appeared in *Tally Ho* #1, and was a short feature starring the character he had created in elementary school, the "Snowman." The work was simply signed "Fritz," his baseball nickname.

"Fritz" Frazetta contributed a number of funny animal and humorous filler drawings to Standard Publishing over the next few years. These drawings, simple as they were, showed the classic elements of figure and design he had been taught at the Brooklyn Academy, and demonstrated some of the first influential elements he had gleaned from the work of Hal Foster, artist of *Tarzan* and *Prince Valiant*.

Even though he was now a professional artist, Frazetta was also young, footloose, and fancy free, and often preferred playing baseball and palling around with his friends (Roy Krenkel, Al Williamson, Angelo Torres, Nick Meglin, and George Woodbridge, known collectively as the "Fleegle Gang") to working. Consequently, he was rarely given assignments on regular titles and worked instead for a host of different publishing houses, usually collaborating with one of his friends to get the job done.

Frazetta made his first attempt at a syndicated feature, albeit unsuccessfully, in 1948. He collaborated with Joe Greene, a writer for Standard, producing *Tiga* on speculation. *The Shining Knight* was his first major continuity work, done as an ongoing back-up for *Adventure Comics* in 1949. *Dan Brand and Tipi* (later collected as *White Indian*) was his second major series, appearing as a seven to eight page backup in *Durango Kid* (published by Magazine Enterprises) between 1949 and 1951.

1952 was to be a pivotal year in Frank Frazetta's career: at this time he developed a dramatic style, moving from an elegant line with little substance to a line full of character, an elemental line brimming with confidence. Early in the year, Frazetta created and drew *Thun'da, King of the Congo*, the story of a Tarzan-like character, in hopes that he might be offered the *Tarzan* syndicated strip. While that never happened, *Thun'da* showcased Frazetta's abilities and helped establish his reputation for heroic fantasy. In 1952, he also worked on several stories for Educational

Comics (EC) and began *Johnny Comet*.

Most Frazetta fans, on seeing the title *Johnny Comet*, imagine a science fiction story with a handsome, muscular hero, voluptuous women, and lush background—all the things that have come to be Frazetta's trademarks. Well, the hero is muscular, there are some voluptuous women, and the backgrounds are detailed, if not lush. But what a surprise to find that this is a story about a race car driver from northern California!

During the late 1940s and early 1950s, auto racing had become a popular passtime, especially in the South and Midwest. At the time there were several syndicated comics which dealt with sports: Ham Fisher's *Joe Palooka* featured a boxer and *Ozark Ike*, by Ray Gotto, was a baseball strip. *Johnny Comet*, another genre strip, was developed to appeal to the growing number of racing fans.

For a while, Peter DePaolo was credited with writing the stories. He had won the Indianapolis 500 in 1925, and many believe his name was added to the strip to lend credence to the racing story-line. Whether or not he ever actually wrote the series is unclear, but Al Williamson, who was there, says Earl Baldwin was the sole author.

Despite the fame and talent of its creators, *Johnny Comet* did not become a highly successful strip. Even at its height it was in limited syndication, never achieving the easy accessibility of many of its contemporaries.

During June 1952, Frazetta's artwork began to lose some of the background detail that had marked the first few months' output. *Johnny Comet*'s "middle age" is more spartan, almost ascetic, in its emphasis on the basics—people and cars. Nevertheless, the drawing *per se* was constantly evolving and growing in confidence until, toward the end of his tenure on *Johnny Comet*, Frazetta began to exhibit the style that would identify him forever after. The beautiful, elegant brushwork found early in the run lacks the strength that eventually developed when Frazetta began putting the pen to more, and better, use. In the final Sunday of the series, the livelier penwork on Pa Bottle's sleeve contrasts with and heightens the liquidity of the brushwork delineating his neck and face. The elevation of the pen from a subordinate role to that of "co-star" adds the final, crowning touch to a style that would, over the course of his remaining years in comics, come to be viewed as quintessential Frazetta.

Sadly, this style was not to grace the comics page for long. It

Unreleased *Sweet Adeline* strip

was not unusual for a newspaper feature of the 1950s to be designed to appear for only a year or so. *Johnny Comet*, although not intended for a short run, joined the ranks of those strips; it lasted only 372 days.

There had been indications of problems with the strip. Initially *Johnny Comet* ran seven days a week; six dailies forming one storyline and the Sundays presenting a different, ongoing story. In August 1952 a change occurred: the daily strip maintained an action-oriented motif, while Sunday's episodes became humorous vignettes featuring the regular characters, but not necessarily relating to the storyline of the day-to-day adventure.

In addition, *Johnny Comet* had changed its name nine months into the run, becoming *Ace McCoy* on November 29, 1952. The new name was chosen by a zealous movie producer, thinking it was more "Hollywood" than *Johnny Comet*. At that point a new writer, Earl Baldwin, was introduced.

These alterations were to no avail. Just when everything was looking promising, the daily sequence ended, between episodes, on January 31, 1953. The last Sunday strip appeared on February 1. Presumably, the series ended because of a lack of subscribers.

Following *Johnny Comet*, Frazetta remained interested in syndicated work. He ghosted Dan Barry's *Flash Gordon* for two weeks in addition to submitting two ideas of his own to newspaper syndicates. *Ambi Dexter* featured a baseball pitcher who could throw either right- or left-handed; the second strip, *Sweet Adeline*, was the story of a young working woman of the '50s. *Nina* was a concept written and drawn by Frazetta somewhat similar to *Thun'da* (except for the fact that Nina was a beautiful blonde), which he hoped to produce as a Sunday-only strip. Unfortunately, none of these ideas were of interest to the syndicates.

In 1953, Frazetta accepted Al Capp's invitation to join the *Li'l Abner* studio, where he was to remain until 1957. Depending on whether one reads the accounts of Capp or Frazetta, Fritz's contribution was either small or immeasurable. Regardless, looking at Frazetta's work from this time, even the casual reader cannot miss the many stylistic and visual contributions Frazetta made to the strip, not the least of which was the frequent addition of feminine pulchritude.

While at Capp's studio, Frazetta worked for other companies, producing his classic Buck Rogers covers for *Famous Funnies*, drawing for *Personal Love*, including the beautiful story "Untamed Love," adding to such wonderful stories as "Fifty Girls Fifty" and "New Beginning" (pencilled by his friend Al Williamson), and drawing the classic EC story "Squeeze Play," his only solo story for EC (although he was assisted by Williamson on many pages).

After leaving the Capp studio, Frazetta worked on a variety of projects, including Jim Warren's fledgling *Creepy* and *Eerie* magazines, providing both covers and "Werewolf!", his last story for comics. He also assisted Harvey Kurtzman on "Little Annie Fannie" for *Playboy* and, oh yes, he did a few paintings.

From this point on, most Frazetta fans are aware of the meteoric rise of his career. With both covers and interior art for Ace's new line of Edgar Rice Burroughs' titles, including *Tarzan*, *Carson of Venus*, and the *Pellucidar* books, Frazetta established himself as a painter and ceased producing continuity. His paintings of Robert E. Howard's Conan solidified his place in fantasy art.

In the years since the publication of *Conan*, Frazetta's style and energy have had a tremendous influence on many fantasy and comics artists, from Jeff Jones, Berni Wrightson, and Michael Kaluta, to Dave Stevens, William Stout, Mark Schultz, Bo Hampton, and Mike Mignola. Undoubtedly, many genera-tions of artists to come will continue the Frazetta tradition.

For many of the master's fans, *Johnny Comet* was just one part of the Frazetta mystique—an auspicious beginning to an illustrious career, a harbinger of his versatility in comics rendition and artistic expression.

Very few people have had the opportunity to read this series in its entirety. For the Frazetta fan and the person who appreciates newspaper strips, this collection of *Johnny Comet-Ace McCoy* is a long-awaited treat. Look at the linework in these panels—look closely at the graceful figures and wonderful faces—and remember that Frank Frazetta was only 24 years old when Johnny Comet ran his brief but spectacular race through America's funny pages.

# DAILY STRIPS

TO SAVE YOUNG SMITH, JOHNNY SMACKS THE KID'S CAR INTO POSITION...

2-1

OH OH! NOW JOHNNY'S IN TROUBLE!

2-2

COMET'S BOUNCED OFF THE RAIL AND IS SPINNING INTO THE PATH OF THE OTHER CARS!

In saving another driver from crashing, Johnny accidentally smacks the rail.. and finds himself in a spin!

2-4

HE'S GOING TO *TURN OVER!*

JOHNNY COMET'S CAR IS CRASHING ON THE FAR TURN!

2-5

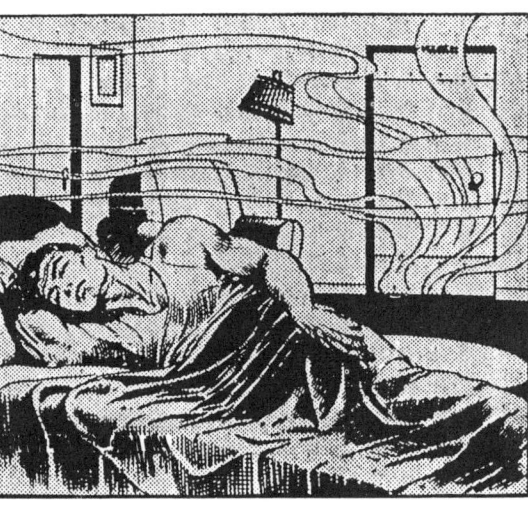

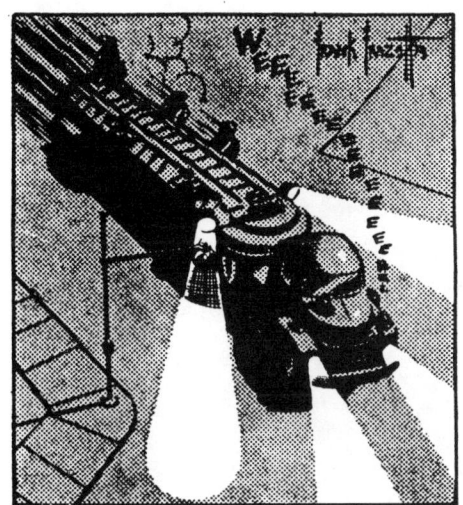

SUSPICIOUS OF AL GORE'S ATTEMPTS TO DESTROY JEAN FARGO'S NEW RACER, JOHNNY CATCHES HIM LEAVING TO KEEP AN APPOINTMENT WITH A MYSTERIOUS MR. BLUE...

3-24

HE'S IN AN AWFUL HURRY... MIGHT BE WORTH- WHILE FOLLOWING HIM.

BLUE GARTER

JOHNNY COMET! AND HE'S FOLLOWING AL!

PALACE HOTEL? CONNECT ME WITH ROOM 203, PLEASE..

WHO WOULD GORE BE WANTING TO SEE IN THAT RATTRAP?

PALACE HOTEL

DON'T JAY-WALK! WHY SAVE TIME YOU MAY NOT LIVE TO USE?

K102

3-25

HELLO, BOSS.

YOU FOOL! JOHNNY COMET'S BEEN FOLLOWING YOU!

QUICK.. HIDE IN THIS CLOSET!

FIREBALL, IN A SUDDEN BLAZE OF SPEED, STARTS TO SQUEEZE INSIDE AS BOTH CARS ROAR WIDE OPEN INTO THE TURN!

4-16

WHAT'S FIREBALL TRYIN' TO DO .. GET SOMEBODY KILLED?

IN HIS DELIBERATE ATTEMPT TO CRACK UP JOHNNY, FIREBALL MISJUDGES HIS SPEED AND BOTH CARS LOCK WHEELS!

TRYING TO CRASH JOHNNY, FIREBALL MISJUDGES HIS SPEED... AND SENDS HIS OWN CAR INTO A LOOP!

4-17

McNaught Syndicate, Inc

FIREBALL'S CAR CRASHES INTO THE INFIELD AND EXPLODES!

GREENPOINT THIS TIME, JEAN, OR BUST!

WE'LL FOLLOW AS SOON AS THE COLONEL'S CAR GETS HERE.

RIGHTO!

5-16

MEANWHILE, IN THE COLONEL'S LIBRARY AT GREENPOINT...

DIDN'T EDDIE WRECK THEM AS I ORDERED?

HE MUFFED IT. COMET'S SAFE AND ON HIS WAY..

ZIP, DARLING, YOU DON'T THINK I'M GOING TO LET COMET REPLACE YOU AS MY FATHER'S RACE DRIVER THIS EASILY, DO YOU?

FRANK FRAZETTA

COMET'S ALL RIGHT...JUST DOESN'T KNOW HE'S COSTING ME A JOB.

KISS ME GOOD-BYE, ZIP... I HAVE SOMETHING TO DO.

FRANK FRAZETTA

...AND THAT SOMETHING CONCERNS MR. COMET.

5-17

EDDIE JUGG, FATHER'S CHAUFFEUR, WILL DO ANYTHING FOR MONEY...

THERE'S A MAN DOWNSTAIRS ...SAYS HIS NAME'S COMET.

5-19

AGAINST RAVEN ROCKETT'S WISHES, HER FATHER HAS HIRED JOHNNY AS HIS NEW RACE DRIVER. WHEN JOHNNY ARRIVES, RAVEN CONCEALS HER DISLIKE OF HIM..

I'M RAVEN ROCKETT.. WELCOME TO GREENPOINT, MR. COMET!

GEE, THANKS, MISS ROCKETT.

FRANK FRAZETTA

I'LL SHOW YOU THE GARAGE... AND PLEASE CALL ME RAVEN.

SOMETHING TELLS ME THIS IS THE BEGINNING OF TROUBLE.

5-20

WOW.. WHAT A GARAGE!

BEING A RACE CAR ENTHUSIAST, FATHER HAD TO HAVE THE BEST.

FRANK FRAZETTA

TEN-TON PRESSURE .. WOW! THIS THING COULD CRUSH A BALL-BEARING INTO A PIECE OF CONFETTI!

IF HE PUTS HIS FINGERS IN IT, I'LL KICK ON THE SWITCH.

5-23

SHE FAINTED ..I CAUGHT HER. THAT'S ALL!

THAT'S ENOUGH!

MEANWHILE, IN THE GARAGE...

COME! I'LL TAKE YOU BOYS TO YOUR QUARTERS.

MEET ME IN THE LIBRARY IN FIVE MINUTES.

WHAT'S UP?

COMET'S GOING TO QUIT THIS JOB.. IF HE WANTS TO LIVE.

5-24

OKAY. WHAT'S THE PROPOSITION?

NEXT WEEK FATHER'S HAVING COMET TRY OUT THE NEW RACER...

...IF COMET WRECKED IT, HE'D HAVE TO RESIGN, GET WHAT I MEAN?

DOG-GONE! I HAVE TO WORK FRIDAY.. JUST WHEN THEY'RE BROADCASTING THE INDIANAPOLIS RACE!

DO YOU HAVE THE FEELING WE'RE BEING WATCHED?

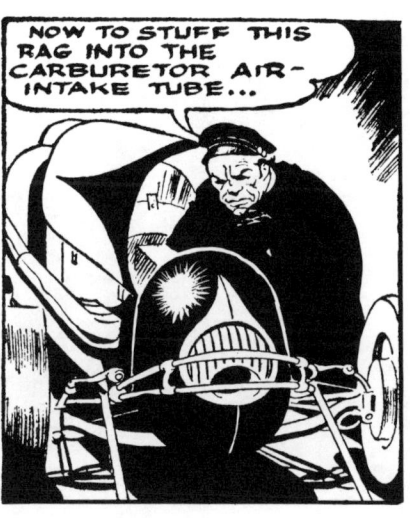

EDDIE JUGG, TO DISCREDIT JOHNNY, HAS SECRETLY TAMPERED WITH THE MIDGET'S ENGINE, CAUSING IT TO CATCH ON FIRE...

6-9

I'M OKAY. HELP POP SAVE THE CAR.

LATER

WE'RE WASHED UP. THE COLONEL'S BOUND TO DISCHARGE US FOR THIS.

... AND THEN IT BLEW OUT A GASKET AND BURST INTO FLAMES.

CONFOUND IT, MAN! THIS WASHES ME RIGHT OUT OF THE CENTINELLA RACE.

6-10

UNDER THE CIRCUMSTANCES, I SUPPOSE I'M DISCHARGED.

MEANWHILE, RAVEN KEEPS A RENDEZVOUS WITH ZIP WILSON...

COMET'S UPSTAIRS NOW, HONEY, BEING FIRED.

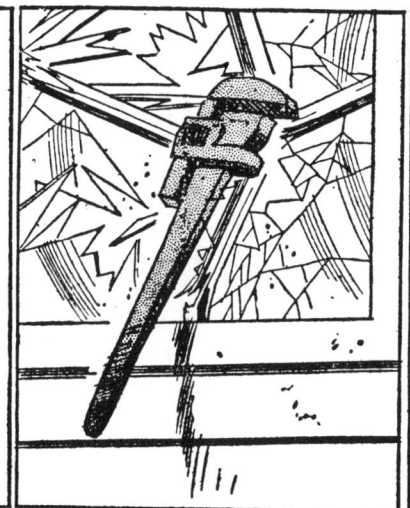

As JOHNNY SPEEDS AWAY WITH IDA, HE IS MOMENTARILY BLINDED BY THE LIGHTS OF AN ARRIVING CAR!

THAT WAS JOHNNY AND *THAT WOMAN!*

QUICK, TELL ME..DID JOHNNY JUST LEAVE WITH IDA?

HE SHORE DID AND *I HELPED*.. SO THIS GUY COULDN'T GET HER:

THEN YOU MUST BE INSANE! LOOK AT THIS PAPER AND SEE *WHO SHE IS!*

At an intersection on highway 101, police have set a road block to intercept the truck in which Johnny is innocently helping an absconding cashier to escape...

THEY OUGHT TO BE COMING ALONG SOON.

JOHNNY, DON'T YOU KNOW A SHORT CUT TO THE STATION?

I COULD TAKE THE OLD RIVER ROAD.. BUT IT'S DANGEROUS IN SPOTS.

THAT'S ALL RIGHT! I DON'T MIND!

McNaught Syndicate, Inc

HERE WE GO! HOLD ON TIGHT!

I TOLD YOU IT WAS A BAD ROAD.

I DON'T CARE! JUST GET ME TO THE RAILROAD!

ROAD CLOSED WASHOUT

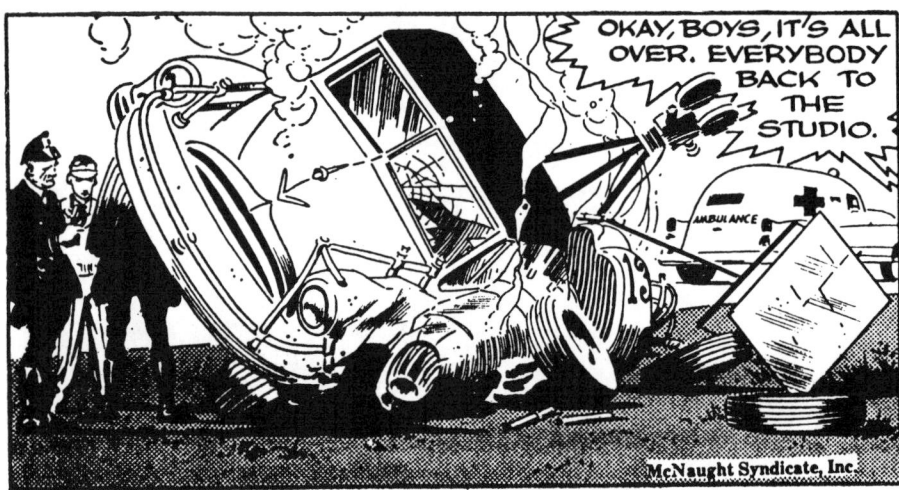

We have been unable to locate a copy of the daily strip for December 12, 1952.

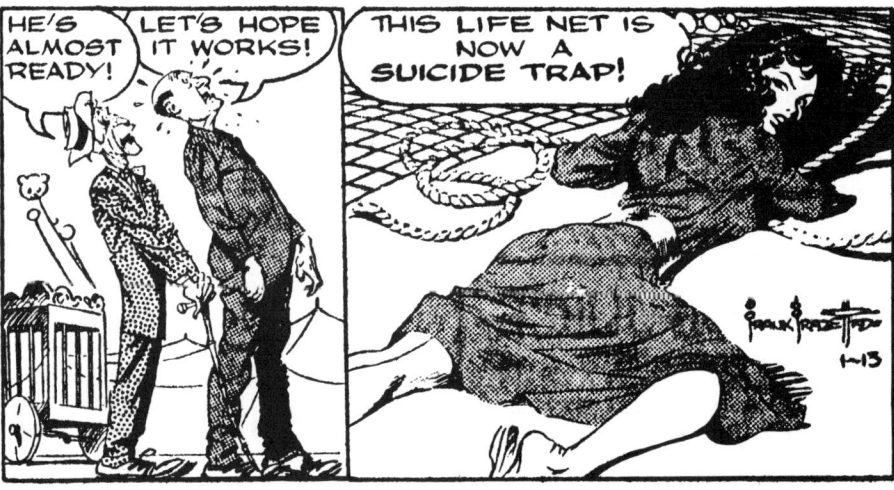

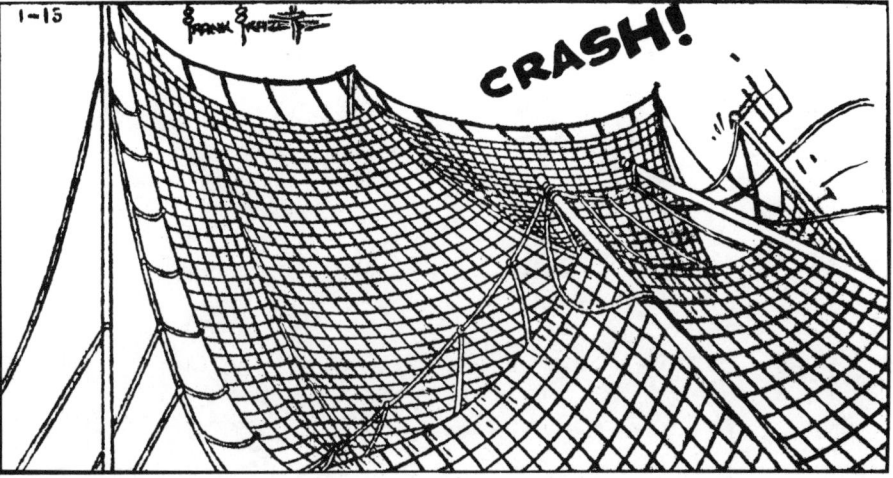

We have been unable to locate a copy of the daily strip for January 20, 1953.

# SUNDAY STRIPS

We have been unable to locate a copy of the Sunday strip for February 10, 1952.

We have been unable to lacate a copy of the Sunday strip for February 17, 1952.

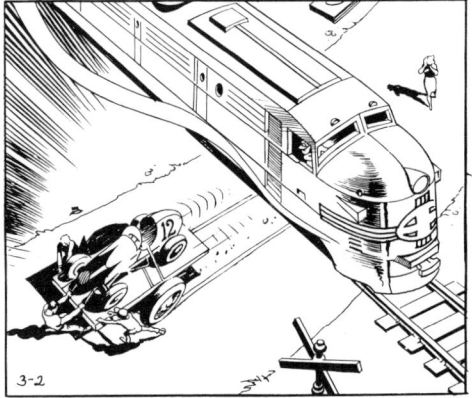

HOPING TO DISCOVER A REASON FOR ITS NUMEROUS CRASHES, JOHNNY AND JEAN INSPECT THE JINXED BROOKVALE SPEEDWAY...

THE TRACK LOOKS IN GOOD CONDITION AND THE TURNS ARE BANKED PROPERLY.

YET WE'VE HAD SO MANY CRACK-UPS LATELY THAT ALL THE TOP-NOTCH DRIVERS ARE QUITTING US.

AND MR. ROE'S GOING BANKRUPT.

ACRES OF PARKING SPACE

THOSE CRASHES AREN'T ACCIDENTS. SOMEBODY'S CAUSING THEM ... AND I'M BEGINNING TO GET AN IDEA WHY!

WHILE LOOKING THE BROOKVALE SPEEDWAY OVER, SOMETHING SUDDENLY AROUSES JOHNNY'S SUSPICIONS...

HOW MANY ACRES OF PARKING SPACE SURROUND THE TRACK AND WHO OWNS THEM?

NINETY ACRES. THEY'RE CHET DRUM'S AND HE LEASES 'EM TO THE TRACK.

3-16

THAT ELIMINATES YOUR SUSPICIONS OF MR. DRUM.

YEAH. HE WOULDN'T WANT THE TRACK TO CLOSE WHEN HE'S MAKING MONEY FROM IT.

MEANWHILE, IN CHET DRUM'S GARAGE WHERE SPARKY HAS BEEN LEFT TO GUARD JOHNNY'S RACER...

WHEN THE SUN GOES DOWN, THIS JOINT'S CHILLY.

I TURN THE GAS OFF ... THE HEATER GOES OUT ... THEN I TURN THE GAS BACK ON.

AND THE CHUMP INSIDE DON'T KNOW THE GAS IS ESCAPING. TERRIFIC!

NOW WE TURN OFF THE METER, AIR THE JOINT OUT ...

... AND CRIPPLE THAT RACER -- BUT GOOD!

BEAT IT, CHET! HERE COMES COMET AND THE FARGO DAME!

WAIT A MINUTE, JEAN. I'LL STRIKE A MATCH.

METER STILL ON AND GAS ESCAPING.

TO BE CONTINUED...

QUESTION BOX

to —

GEORGE FREYTAG WEST ORANGE, N.J.

THE AVERAGE WHEELBASE FOR A MIDGET RACE CAR IS 85 INCHES.

FORMER INDIANAPOLIS CHAMPION

SENSING JOHNNY COMET IS APPEARING AT BROOKVALE SPEEDWAY TO UNRAVEL THE MYSTERY OF ITS NUMEROUS CRASHES, A HUGE CROWD TURNS OUT FOR THE BIG RACE...

—50 LAP—
FEATURE RACE TONIGHT

BROOKVALE – SPEEDWAY – BR

COMET, IN CAR NO. 12, HAS JUST QUALIFIED AT 13.8.

JOHNNY'S QUALIFYING SPEED PLEASES CHET DRUM, LOCAL REALTOR, WHO OCCUPIES HIS USUAL BOX AT THE SOUTH TURN...

COMET GETS THE POLE POSITION.

THAT'S WHERE ALL THE CRASHES HAPPEN, AIN'T IT, CHET?

THEY'RE OFF!

STARTING THE 26TH LAP, COMET IN CAR NO. 12 IS NOW TAKING THE LEAD!

LOOK AT JOHNNY GO!

HE'S PASSING NO. 3 GOING INTO THE TURN!

BUT SUDDENLY A SEARING FLASH OF LIGHT BLINDS JOHNNY...

MOMENTARILY BLINDED, JOHNNY LOSES CONTROL OF HIS CAR...

TO BE CONTINUED...

QUESTION BOX

to

REV. ALAN CHEESEBRO
SHERMAN OAKS, CALIF.

BEING SO FAMILIAR WITH THE HAZARDS OF SPEED, RACE DRIVERS ARE INSTINCTIVELY CAUTIOUS WHEN DRIVING ON PUBLIC HIGHWAYS.

Peter DePaolo

FORMER INDIANAPOLIS CHAMPION

**?**

WHAT'S THE MATTER, NURSE?

THAT'S STRANGE. I'M SURE I LEFT A PITCHER OF WATER ON THAT TABLE.

FOR SOME MYSTERIOUS REASON, TRIXIE WANTS TO DISPOSE OF JIM REYNOLDS, INJURED MOTORDROME OWNER. SHE HAS SECRETLY POISONED A PITCHER OF WATER, WHEN...

THAT'S STALE. I'LL GET SOME FRESH WATER WHILE THE DOCTOR EXAMINES MR. REYNOLDS.

THEY'LL WANT SOME PRIVACY. COMING, MR. COMET?

HOW DID YOU KNOW MY NAME?

I KNEW JIM SENT FOR YOU. I'M TRIXIE, HIS TICKET SELLER AT THE PARK.

EXIT →

4-27

JIM NEEDS CASH... I'VE **GOT** TO RE-OPEN HIS MOTORDROME.

HIRING ANOTHER TRICK MOTOR-CYCLE DRIVER WOULD BREAK YOU.

I'VE GOT IT! I'LL DRIVE A **MIDGET RACER** UP THE WALLS OF THAT BARREL!

I'LL EXAMINE THE CONSTRUCTION OF THE MOTORDROME RIGHT NOW ... THEN WIRE MISS FARGO.

SMART IDEA... GOOD NIGHT.

SURF HOTE

LATER

COMET'S STILL INSIDE, JOE.

McNaught Syndicate, Inc.

COME DOWN, YOU FOOL! WHEN THIS BOLT COMES OFF, THE WHOLE TOP SECTION'S GONNA CAVE IN!

TO BE CONTINUED...

QUESTION BOX

to —
MRS. BEN JOLLEY
DALLAS, TEXAS

CERTAINLY WE WELCOME QUERIES FROM THE LADIES! RACING CARS ARE **NOT** EQUIPPED WITH RADIATOR FANS.

*Peter DePaolo*

FORMER INDIANAPOLIS CHAMPION

UNKNOWN ENEMIES ARE TRYING TO PREVENT JOHNNY FROM RE-OPENING JIM REYNOLDS' MOTORDROME AND HE HAS SENT FOR JEAN AND SPARKY...

WE LEFT AS SOON AS WE GOT YOUR TELEGRAM.

WHAT'S UP, JOHNNY?

PLENTY...

JIM ASKED ME TO RE-OPEN HIS MOTORDROME TILL HE GETS WELL.. AND SOMEBODY'S TRYING TO STOP ME.

BUT WHY DO YOU WANT THE RACER?

LET'S FIND A QUIET SPOT AND I'LL TELL YOU...

MEANWHILE, IN THE HULA-HULA SHOW NEXT DOOR...

NOW WHAT?

WE GOTTA ACT FAST, JOE, OR WE'RE DEAD!

...AND THEY BROUGHT COMET'S RACER WITH THEM.

WONDER WHAT THEY'RE GONNA PULL!

FRANK FRAZETTA

5-11

...BUT RACING A CAR AROUND THE WALL!

IT'LL DRAW BIG CROWDS, JEAN.

UNTIE THAT END! IT'LL DROP RIGHT ON 'EM.

WAIT, TRIXIE! I GOT A BETTER IDEA.

TO BE CONTINUED...

QUESTION BOX

to —

GEORGE LAMB JR.
VALLEJO, CALIF.

TORSION BARS HAVE REPLACED SEMI-ELLIPTIC SPRINGS ON RACE CARS.

Peter DePaolo

FORMER INDIANAPOLIS CHAMPION

QUESTION BOX

to—
CHARLES PFAFF
WEST ORANGE, N.J.

A FORD ENTRY FINISHED IN 5TH PLACE AT INDIANAPOLIS IN THE 1923 RACE.

Peter DePaolo

FORMER INDIANAPOLIS CHAMPION

We have been unable to locate a copy of the Sunday strip for January 11, 1953.

While every attempt has been made to provide
a complete and well-reproduced collection
of *Johnny Comet,* some strips have eluded us and others
were available only in the form of degenerated copies.
If you can loan us any of the missing strips or can provide
better copies of poor quality strips, please contact us at
P.O. Box 1099, Forestville, California, 95436
so that we may eventually publish
a still more complete *Johnny Comet* collection.

# GRAPHIC ALBUMS FROM ECLIPSE

1. SABRE by Don McGregor and Paul Gulacy
   (1978) 48 pp, 8 1/2 x 11, b&w
   ☐ 1st edition saddle stitched paperback: 20.00
   ☐ 10th Ann. edition trade paperback: 6.95
   ☐ 10th Ann. ed. signed limited cloth: 25.95
2. NIGHT MUSIC by P. Craig Russell
   (1979) 48 pp, 8 1/2 x 11, b&w
   ☐ saddle stitched paperback: 10.00
3. DETECTIVES, INC. by Don McGregor and Marshall Rogers
   (1980) 48 pp, 8 1/2 x 11, b&w
   ☐ trade paperback: 10.00
4. STEWART THE RAT by Steve Gerber, Gene Colan,
   and Tom Palmer
   (1980) 48 pp, 8 1/2 x 11, b&w
   ☐ trade paperback: 8.00
5. THE PRICE by Jim Starlin
   (1981) 48 pp, 8 1/2 x 11, b&w
   ☐ saddle stitched paperback: 25.00
6. I AM COYOTE by Steve Englehart and Marshall Rogers
   (1984) 64 pp, 8 1/2 x 11, full colour
   ☐ trade paperback: 25.00
7. THE ROCKETEER by Dave Stevens
   (1985) 72 pp, 8 1/2 x 11 full colour
   ☐ 2nd printing trade paperback: 8.95
   ☐ 2nd printing clothbound: 20.95
8. ZORRO IN OLD CALIFORNIA by Nedaud and Marcello
   (1986) 64 pp, 8 1/2 x 11, full colour
   ☐ trade paperback: 7.95
   ☐ hardbound: 12.95
9. THE SACRED AND THE PROFANE by Ken Steacy
   and Dean Motter
   (1987) 128 pp, 8 1/2 x 11, full colour
   ☐ trade paperback: 15.95
   ☐ clothbound: 25.95
   ☐ clothbound signed limited edition: 36.00
10. SOMERSET HOLMES by Bruce Jones, April Campbell,
    and Brent Anderson
    (1987) 128 pp, 8 1/2 x 11, full colour
    ☐ trade paperback: 15.95
    ☐ clothbound: 25.95
    ☐ clothbound signed limited edition: 36.00
11. FLOYD FARLAND, CITIZEN OF THE FUTURE by Chris Ware
    (1987) 48 pp, 7 x 10, b&w
    ☐ trade paperback: 3.95
12. SILVERHEELS by Bruce Jones, Scott Hampton,
    and April Campbell
    (1987) 64 pp, 8 1/2 x 11, full colour
    ☐ trade paperback: 8.95
    ☐ hardbound: 15.95
    ☐ hardbound signed limited edition: 25.95
13. THE SISTERHOOD OF STEEL by Christy Marx
    and Peter Ledger
    (1987) 72 pp, 8 1/2 x 11, full colour
    ☐ trade paperback: 9.95
    ☐ clothbound: 15.95
    ☐ clothbound signed limited edition: 25.95
14. SAMURAI, SON OF DEATH by Sharman DiVono
    and Hiroshi Hirata
    (1987) 48 pp, 7 x 10, b&w
    ☐ trade paperback: 4.95

15. AIR FIGHTERS CLASSICS edited by Catherine Yronwode
    (1987—1989) 64 pp, 7x 10, b&w, trade paperback
    ☐ Vol. 1: The Origin of Airboy: 4.95
    ☐ Vol. 2: The Origin of Skywolf: 4.95
    ☐ Vol. 3: Secrets of the Bird Plane: 4.95
    ☐ Vol. 4: Bombs Over Boston: 4.95
    ☐ Vol. 5: Blasting Berlin to Bits: 4.95
16. TWISTED TALES edited by Bruce Jones and April Campbell
    (1987) 48 pp, 7 x 10, full colour
    ☐ trade paperback: $4.95
17. VALKYRIE, PRISONER OF THE PAST by Charles Dixon,
    Paul Gulacy, and Will Blyberg
    (1988) 76 pp, 7 x 10, full colour
    ☐ trade paperback: 7.95
    ☐ clothbound signed limited edition: 30.95
18. SCOUT: THE FOUR MONSTERS by Timothy Truman
    and Thomas Yeates
    (1988) 136 pp, 7 x 10, full colour
    ☐ trade paperback: 15.95
    ☐ clothbound signed limited edition: 36.00
19. XYR by Stuart Hopen, Ben Dunn, Frank Giacoia,
    and Jim Mooney
    (1988) 48 pp, 7 x 10, b&w
    ☐ trade paperback: 4.95
20. ALIEN WORLDS edited by Bruce Jones and
    April Campbell
    (1988) 48 pp, 7 x 10, full colour
    ☐ trade paperback: 4.95
21. HEARTBREAK COMICS by David Boswell
    (1988) 48 pp, 8 1/2 x 11, b&w
    ☐ trade paperback: 5.95
22. ALEX TOTH'S ZORRO by Alex Toth
    (1988) 120 pp, 8 1/2 x 11, b&w
    ☐ Vol. 1 trade paperback: 10.95
    ☐ Vol. 2 trade paperback: 10.95
    ☐ clothbound vols. 1 and 2 signed limited edition,
      together in one slipcase: 55.00
23. SHE by H. Rider Haggard
    adapted by Dick Davis and Vincent Napoli
    (1988) 64 pp, 7 x 10, b&w
    ☐ trade paperback: 5.95
24. BROUGHT TO LIGHT by Alan Moore, Bill Sienkiewicz,
    Joyce Brabner, Thomas Yeates, and Paul Mavrides
    (1988) 80 pp, 8 1/2 x 11, b&w
    ☐ trade paperback: 9.95
    ☐ clothbound: 30.95
25. MIRACLEMAN: BOOK ONE by Alan Moore,
    Garry Leach, and Alan Davis
    (1988) 80 pp, 7 x 10, full colour
    ☐ trade paperback: 10.95
    ☐ clothbound: 30.95
26. REAL LOVE: The Best of the Simon & Kirby
    Romance Comics edited by Richard Howell
    (1988) 160 pp, 8 1/2 x 11, b&w
    ☐ trade paperback: 13.95
27. PIGEONS FROM HELL by Robert E. Howard
    Adapted by Scott Hampton
    (1988) 64 pp, 8 1/2 x 11, full colour
    ☐ trade paperback: 8.95
    ☐ clothbound signed limited edition: 30.95

28. TEENAGED DOPE SLAVES & REFORM SCHOOL
    GIRLS edited by Dean Mullaney
    (1988) 112 pp, 8 1/2 x 11, b&w
    ☐ trade paperback: 10.95
29. BOGIE by Claude Jean-Philippe and Patrick Lesueur
    (1988) 64 pp, 8 1/2 x 11, full colour
    ☐ trade paperback: 10.95
30. ARIANE AND BLUEBEARD by Maurice Maeterlinck
    adapted by P. Craig Russell
    (1988) 48 pp, 7 x 10, full colour
    ☐ trade paperback: 4.95
    ☐ clothbound signed limited edition: 30.95
31. INTO THE SHADOW OF THE SUN: RAEL by Colin Wilson
    (1988) 48 pp, 8 1/2 x 11, full colour
    ☐ trade paperback: 8.95
32. KRAZY & IGNATZ by George Herriman
    (1988—1990) 64 pp, 9 x 12,b7w
    ☐ Vol. 1: 1916 trade paperback: 10.95
    ☐ Vol. 1: 1916 limited clothbound: 30.95
    ☐ Vol. 2: 1917 trade paperback: 10.95
    ☐ Vol. 2: 1917 limited clothbound: 30.95
    ☐ Vol. 3: 1918 trade paperback: 10.95
    ☐ Vol. 3: 1918 limited clothbound: 30.95
    ☐ Vol. 4: 1919 trade paperback: 10.95
    ☐ Vol. 4: 1919 limited clothbound: 30.95
    ☐ Vol. 5: 1920 trade paperback: 10.95
    ☐ Vol. 5: 1920 limited clothbound: 30.95
    ☐ Vol. 6: 1921 trade paperback: 10.95
    ☐ Vol. 6: 1921 limited clothbound: 30.95
    ☐ Vol. 7: 1922 trade paperback: 10.95
    ☐ Vol. 7: 1922 limited clothbound: 30.95
33. DR WATCHSTOP: ADVENTURES IN TIME AND SPACE
    by Ken Macklin
    (1989) 64 pp, 8 1/2 x 11, full colour
    ☐ trade paperback: 8.95
    ☐ clothbound signed limited edition: 30.95
34. JAMES BOND 007: LICENSE TO KILL by Mike Grell
    Chuck Austen, Thomas Yeates, & Stan Woch
    (1989) 48 pp, 8 1/2 x 11, full colour
    ☐ trade paperback: 8.95
    ☐ clothbound: 30.95
35. TAPPING THE VEIN by Clive Barker
    illustrated by Craig Russell, Scott Hampton, Klaus Janson,
    John Bolton, Bo Hampton, and Denys Cowan
    (1989—90) 48 pp each, 7 x 10, full colour
    ☐ Book 1 trade paperback: 7.95
    ☐ Book 2 trade paperback: 7.95
    ☐ Book 3 trade paperback: 7.95
36. SCOUT: MOUNT FIRE by Timothy Truman
    (1989) 148 pp, 7 x 10, full colour
    ☐ trade paperback: 10.95
    ☐ clothbound signed limited edition: 30.95
37. TOADSWART D'AMPLESTONE by Tim Conrad
    (1989) 122 pp, 8 1/2 x 11, b&w
    ☐ trade paperback: 13.95
    ☐ clothbound signed limited edition: 36.00
38. LARRY MARDER'S BEANWORLD by Larry Marder
    (1989) 122 pp, 7 x 10, b&w
    ☐ trade paperback: 10.95
    ☐ clothbound signed limited edition: 30.95

39. POGO & ALBERT by Walt Kelly
    (1989) 64 pp, 8 1/2 x 11, full colour
    ☐ Vol. 1 trade paperback: 9.95
    ☐ Vol. 1 limited clothbound: 30.95
    ☐ Vol. 2 trade paperback: 9.95
    ☐ Vol. 2 limited clothbound: 30.95
    ☐ Vol. 3 trade paperback: 9.95
    ☐ Vol. 3 limited clothbound: 30.95
    ☐ Vol. 4 trade paperback: 9.95
    ☐ Vol. 4 limited clothbound: 30.95
40. THE RETURN OF VALKYRIE by Tim Truman,
    Chuck Dixon, Tom Yeates, Stan Woch & Will Blyberg
    (1989) 88 pp, 7 x 10, full colour
    ☐ trade paperback: 10.95
    ☐ clothbound signed limited edition: 30.95
41. THE HOBBIT by J. R. R. Tolkien
    adapted by Charles Dixon and David Wenzel
    (1990) 152 pp, 7 x 10, full colour
    ☐ trade paperback: 13.95
    ☐ clothbound: 40.95
    ☐ clothbound signed limited edition: 126.00
42. APPLESEED: THE PROMETHEAN CHALLENGE
    by Masamune Shirow
    adapted by Dana Lewis and Toren Smith
    (1990) 192 pp, 7 x 10, b&w
    ☐ trade paperback: 12.95
    ☐ clothbound signed limited edition: 45.00
43. DIRTY PAIR: BIOHAZARDS by Toren Smith and Adam Warren
    (1990) 112 pp, 7 x 10, b&w
    ☐ trade paperback: 9.95
    ☐ clothbound signed limited edition: 35.00
44. WHAT'S MICHAEL? by Mikoto Kobayashi
    (1990) 128 pp, 7 x 10, b&w
    ☐ trade paperback: 10.95
    ☐ clothbound limited edition: 30.95
45. THE MAGIC FLUTE adapted by P. Craig Russell
    from the opera by Wolfgang Amadeus Mozart
    (1990) 48 pp. each, 7 x 10, full color
    ☐ Vol. 1 trade paperback: 5.95
    ☐ Vol. 2 trade paperback: 5.95
    ☐ Vol. 3 trade paperback: 5.95
46. ORBIT: The Best of Isaac Asimov's Science Fiction Magazine
    edited by Letitia Glozer
    (1990) 48 pp. each, 7 x 10, full colour
    ☐ Vol. 1 trade paperback: 5.95
    ☐ Vol. 2 trade paperback: 5.95
47. THE BLACK TERROR: Seduction of Deceit
    by Beau Smith, Charles Dixon, and Dan Brereton
    (1990) 48 pp. each, 7 x 10, full color
    ☐ Vol. 1 trade paperback: 5.95
    ☐ Vol. 2 trade paperback: 5.95
    ☐ Vol. 3 trade paperback: 5.95

SEND TWO FIRST CLASS STAMPS FOR A COMPLETE CATALOGUE OF
ECLIPSE GRAPHIC ALBUMS,
BOOKS, COMICS, TRADING CARDS, AND RECORDS.
ECLIPSE BOOKS, P. O. BOX 1099,
FORESTVILLE, CALIFORNIA 95436